mary-kateandashley

so little time

Check out these other great

so little time

titles:

mary-kateandashley
so little time

surf holiday

By Nancy Butcher

Based on the series created by Eric Cohen
and Tonya Hurley

HarperCollins*Entertainment*
An Imprint of HarperCollins*Publishers*

A PARACHUTE PRESS BOOK

A PARACHUTE PRESS BOOK

Parachute Publishing, L.L.C.
156 Fifth Avenue
Suite 302
NEW YORK
NY 10010

First published in the USA by HarperEntertainment 2004
First published in Great Britain by HarperCollins*Entertainment* 2005
HarperCollins*Entertainment* is an imprint of HarperCollins*Publishers* Ltd,
77-85 Fulham Palace Road, Hammersmith, London W6 8JB

The HarperCollins *Children's Books* website address is
www.harpercollins.co.uk

1 3 5 7 9 10 8 6 4 2

The authors assert the moral right to be
identified as the authors of the work.

ISBN 0-00-720480-9

Printed and bound in Great Britain by Clays Ltd, St Ives plc

chapter
one

"Those are the cutest ski jackets I have ever seen!" Chloe Carlson exclaimed to her sister, Riley. "I think we should each get one."

Fourteen-year-old Chloe pictured herself in the orange jacket that Riley was holding up. No, the silver one would look better with her hair. Of course, she and Riley had the exact same shade of blond hair, not to mention the same blue eyes and the same complexion. Still, Chloe thought that the silver jacket suited her personality better.

Riley laughed. "That's a great idea. Except we came to the mall to do some last-minute Christmas shopping, remember? For other people?"

"Fine. I'll buy you the orange jacket for Christmas, and you can buy me the silver one. They're only—" Chloe paused to check out the price tag. She let out a small scream when she saw the triple digits. "Aargh! I mean, they're a tiny bit more expensive than I thought."

"Maybe we should wait for the January sales," Riley suggested.

"But we're leaving for Vail on Saturday!" Chloe groaned. "We have everything else we need . . . new snowboards, hats and scarves, the coolest sunglasses. But we still need the perfect jackets. And these jackets are really special." She grinned. "They have personal stereo systems inside with headphones sewn into the hoods. We could listen to our fave CDs while we tear up moguls."

Chloe and Riley were leaving for Vail, Colorado, in just three days. Their mother, Macy, was taking them to the famous ski resort for their holiday vacation. Chloe couldn't wait to hit the slopes with her new snowboard.

And she couldn't wait to see snow. At home in Malibu, California, there was nothing but sunshine and warm, balmy weather almost 365 days a year. Which was nothing to complain about. Still, there was something special about seeing snowflakes falling gently onto a pure white landscape.

The three of them also planned to visit the resort's spa for lots of postskiing massages and beauty treatments. Chloe had read online that the spa's pineapple-papaya facials were to die for.

"Let's go next door to Video Planet and get some DVDs for Dad," Riley said, tucking her arm through Chloe's. "That will get our minds off the—hey, look at those awesome black ski pants!"

"Oh, we *have* to get them!" Chloe cried out.

Ten minutes and lots of cash transactions later—the pants *were* thirty percent off after all—Chloe and Riley managed to tear themselves away from Powder-hounds.

They stopped to look at a flyer for Surf Expo posted on the wall outside the door. "I guess we're going to miss that when we go to Vail," Riley said sadly.

"I know you've been looking forward to it since last year, but trust me . . . once you hit the slopes, you won't miss it at all," Chloe said as they turned to go into Video Planet.

Chloe shifted her shopping bag from one arm to the other as she scanned the shelves of DVDs. "So what would Dad like?"

Riley pointed to several titles and read them out loud. "*Beach Yoga for Your Health. The Meat-Free Gourmet. Spirituality After Forty.*"

Chloe pretended to yawn. "Okay. As long as we don't have to watch them with him when we stay over at his place."

[Chloe: See, Mom and Dad are separated. They decided to split up when they realized that they live at two different speeds. You know the story of the tortoise and the hare? Well, Dad is the tortoise; Mom is the hare—on caffeine. Riley and I live with Mom in our beach house in Malibu. Dad decided he

preferred the simple life in his small trailer by
the ocean. He's into yoga, meditation, and
health foods with strange names.]

Riley grinned and put the three DVDs into a
shopping basket. The sisters continued to browse.
Riley found some movies for her best friend, Sierra.
Chloe found a special three-DVD set for her
boyfriend, Lennon, of his favorite TV show. It cost
more than she had wanted to spend, but Lennon was
so worth it.

"Hey, Chloe! What are you doing here?"

Chloe's head flew up at the sound of the familiar
voice.

Lennon was standing in front of her.

Chloe stifled a gasp and whipped the DVD set
behind her back.

[**Chloe**: Okay, this is what you call bad timing.
Did Lennon see my present for him? Did I blow
his big Christmas surprise?]

Lennon leaned to kiss her. Chloe noticed that he
was holding something behind his back, too.

"Hi, Lennon," Chloe said, enjoying the kiss. "What
are *you* doing here?"

"Uh—just picking out some DVDs for my mom,"
Lennon said quickly.

"That's what we're doing, too! We're picking out
some DVDs for our dad," Chloe said. "No one else. Just
our dad."

"That's cool," Lennon said. "Hey, Riley."

"Hey, Lennon," Riley said with a little wave.

Lennon turned back to Chloe. "Listen, I was going to call you. Are you free Friday night? Do you want to go out with me and my parents? We want to take you out for a special good-bye dinner before you leave for Vail."

"I'd love to," Chloe said eagerly. "Is this going to be fancy or casual?"

"Definitely fancy," Lennon replied. "I'll call you about it later, okay?"

"Okay."

Lennon gave her another kiss, then took off. Chloe noticed him quickly shifting whatever he had been holding behind his back so that she couldn't see it.

"Did you catch what he's getting for me?" Chloe whispered to Riley.

Riley laughed and shook her head. "No! Even if I did, I wouldn't tell you."

Chloe laughed, too. "What kind of sister are you?" she teased. "Anyway, we'd better knock some more stuff off our shopping list or we'll be here all night."

"Slumber party at the mall. Doesn't sound so bad," Riley remarked.

"True," Chloe agreed.

"Okay, check out my snowboarding technique," Riley called out to her sister.

Chloe made a face. "Huh? In case you haven't noticed, we're in Malibu. In our living room. And it's seventy degrees outside."

"You are *such* a skeptic. Watch and learn from the master!"

Riley walked to the hall closet and got out her trusty old surfboard. Then she put it on the living room floor and stepped onto it. Bending her knees slightly, she extended her arms for balance and began swaying back and forth, as though she were zooming down a double-black-diamond slope.

"Okay. You have officially lost your mind," Chloe said, giggling.

Riley giggled, too. She knew that she looked like a freak, especially since she was wearing her brand-new black ski pants with the tags still on them—with a pink tank top and bare feet! But she was really excited about their upcoming trip to Vail. She couldn't wait to glide down a mountain of pure, white, frosty snow with a brisk winter wind whipping through her hair. She wanted to brush up on her snowboarding skills— even if it was on the wrong kind of board and in her living room in Malibu!

Just then the phone rang. Chloe reached over to the coffee table and picked up the phone.

"Hello? Oh, hey." Chloe covered the mouthpiece. "Oh, Ms. Snowboarding Queen, it's for you! It's Charlie."

Riley stepped off her board. Charlie was her boyfriend—i.e., her fave guy in the entire world.

Riley took the phone from Chloe. "Hey," she said happily.

"Hey. What are you doing?"

Riley glanced at her surfboard. "You don't want to know. What are *you* doing?"

"I was just thinking about how much I'm going to miss you while you're in Vail."

Riley's heart melted. Charlie was so sweet. "I'm going to miss you, too," she said softly. "I wish I could clone myself! Then I could go to Vail and stay here with you at the same time. We could hang out and have movie-fests at my house. Or we could hang out at *your* house and have movie-fests there," she added. She had never been to his house. In fact, she hadn't met most of his family.

"Yeah, that would be so great," Charlie agreed.

Then Riley had a sudden inspiration. "Hey! I'm free now. I mean, like, an hour from now, after Chloe and I wrap the bazillion Christmas presents we bought today," she said, catching her sister's glare. "Maybe I could come over?"

"Uh, no . . . I mean . . . why don't I come to your house instead?" Charlie said quickly.

Riley frowned. This was the third or fourth time this had happened. Whenever she suggested that she go to his house, he'd insist on coming to *her* house instead.

But she didn't want to be pushy. "Um, sure," she said. "See you at, like, four?"

"Great. I'll see you then."

"Bye."

"Bye."

"Okay, let's get to work. We have major wrapping to do," Chloe said as soon as Riley hung up. "And if you have time before your love bunny comes over, I need you to help me pick out something to wear Friday night."

[Riley: Love bunny?]

"You mean for your big date with Lennon and his parents?" she said out loud. "It sounds like they're going to take you someplace really fancy. Are you nervous?"

"Not really, I've met his parents lots of times," Chloe said.

"You are so lucky," Riley said. "Lennon's a great guy. Charlie's great too, but I haven't even met his family. Except for his dad, and that was at his alternative CD store, not at their house."

"I'm sure it'll happen soon," Chloe said sympathetically.

"You know your relationship is rock solid when a guy introduces you to his parents." Riley sighed. "So why haven't I met Charlie's family? Does this mean we're not rock solid?"

"You're worrying way too much," Chloe said, grabbing a roll of shiny red paper. "Come on, get into the Christmas spirit! We have tons of wrapping to do, and we can start packing—"

8

She was interrupted by the sound of the front door opening. Car keys jingled. High heels tapped briskly across the floor. It was their mother, Macy.

Macy Carlson walked into the living room. Riley thought her mom looked even more harried than usual. She was talking into two cell phones at once, one at each ear. Her white business suit had a big coffee stain down the front of it.

"Yes, yes, get me on the twelve-fifteen," Macy barked into one of the phones. "No, that order is going to have to wait. Something's come up," she barked into the other one.

Riley and Chloe exchanged a glance. What's up with Mom? Riley wondered.

Macy clicked off both phones and smiled apologetically at her daughters. "Hello, sweeties," she said. "I'm afraid I have some bad news."

"Chloe is cooking dinner tonight?" Riley joked. Chloe threw a pillow at her, which Riley ducked.

"No." Their mother frowned. She looked upset. "I'm so sorry to have to tell you this, but our trip to Vail is off!"

chapter
two

Riley sat there, stunned. Their holiday trip to Vail couldn't be cancelled. Not after all their planning. They had made appointments for massages and facials. They had gone online to find the best restaurants and dance clubs in Vail. Riley had even spent extra time surfing, in the hopes that it would help improve her snowboarding technique. Surely this is a bad joke, she thought, waiting for the punch line. Mom can have a weird sense of humor.

Chloe started cracking up. She obviously had the exact same thoughts. "Right. Very funny, Mom."

Their mother smiled sadly. "I'm afraid I'm not kidding. We're not going to Vail."

[Riley: I have the urge to let out a big primal scream. But that might upset Mom, so I think I'll stifle it. Besides, maybe there's an explanation.]

"Were all the resorts in Vail totally booked or something?" Riley said hopefully. "That's okay, Mom. We can go to Aspen instead. Or Alta. Or Breckenridge. Or even Switzerland! I'll brush up on my French . . . or Italian . . . or German or whatever."

"That's not the problem, girls." Their mom sighed. She plunked herself down on the couch and kicked off her high heels. "Remember my great-aunt Rose? The one who lives in Portland, Oregon?"

Riley nodded. She had met Rose Diggory years ago, when she was five or six, on a family trip to Washington and Oregon. All she could remember of the elderly woman was her small dusty house filled with antiques . . . and cats. Lots and lots of cats. Riley and Chloe had spent the entire visit playing with the felines while their mom complained about all the fur getting on her black designer clothes.

"I just got the word that poor Aunt Rose broke her hip," Macy went on. "She needs someone to take care of her. I'm going to fly up there tomorrow."

"That's awful!" Chloe exclaimed.

"Is she going to be okay?" Riley asked her.

Macy nodded. "Her doctor says she's going to be fine . . . in time. She just can't move around for a while. She needs around-the-clock care."

"What about her son, what's-his-name?" Riley asked. "Doesn't he live in Portland?"

"Douglas. He's in the Australian outback doing a research project. He's going to come home as soon as

11

he can. But in the meantime I'm her only other relative," Macy explained.

"Wow," Riley said.

She moved to the couch and sat down next to her mother. Chloe sat down on the other side. Macy wrapped her arms around both of her daughters. "I'm sorry, girls," she said softly. "I know you're both disappointed."

Riley didn't say anything. She *was* disappointed. But she knew her mother was doing the right thing.

Still, just hours ago she and Chloe had been happily shopping for skiwear at Powderhounds and dreaming about hot-tubbing outside in the icy cold. Now all that was gone. They would be playing in the sand and surf instead of on powdery white slopes. They would be spending their holiday in . . .

"Mom?" Riley said suddenly. "Does this mean we'll be having Christmas this year in Portland? At Aunt Rose's house?"

"No, that's not a good idea," Macy replied. "Her house is too small. There's nowhere for the two of you to sleep. Besides, I don't think we'll be doing a lot of holiday merrymaking, with her in her condition."

Riley and Chloe exchanged a glance. "So that means . . . " Chloe began.

"You'll be spending Christmas with your father," Macy finished.

12

"Oh," Riley and Chloe said in unison.

[Riley: It's not that we don't want to spend Christmas with Dad. It's just that Christmas in Dad's tiny trailer by the ocean is about as far as you can get from a glamorous white Christmas in Vail and still be on the same planet!]

One of Macy's cell phones began to ring. "Excuse me," she said, rising to her feet. "Hello? No, I *don't* want a flight that connects in Dallas! Can't you get me a nonstop out of—"

Chloe leaned over to Riley, looking completely bummed out. "So much for our glam ski vacation," she whispered.

"So much for chestnuts roasting on an open fire," Riley whispered back.

"And pineapple-papaya facials."

"And cute snowboarding instructors."

"Christmas in Dad's trailer." Chloe sighed. "What do you think we'll have for Christmas dinner? Vegetarian chili? Rice cakes with low-fat tofu spread?"

"Hey, look on the bright side," Riley said.

"What bright side?" Chloe asked her.

"What bright side? Well . . . you won't have to be away from Lennon for a whole week," Riley pointed out.

"That's true," Chloe agreed. "And you won't have to be away from Charlie. We'll also get to hang out with our friends. Except Tara and Quinn are going on vacation with their families."

"True," Riley said. "And Larry and Sierra have zillions of relatives visiting, so they won't have a lot of time to hang out."

Focus on the positive, Riley told herself. She would be able to spend lots of time with Charlie. And she would definitely get to meet his mother and sister now. After all, holidays were about family, right?

She could also go surfing every day, she thought, eyeing her surfboard parked on the living room floor. It wasn't the kind of boarding she'd had in mind for her Christmas break, but it would be fun nevertheless. She would become an ace surfer. She would try to convince Charlie to give it a try, too. He had never surfed in his life.

And now that she would be around during the days after Christmas, she could attend the really cool Surf Expo! With the coolest surfing gear and fashions, it was a must-see for surfers in Malibu.

"What's Dad always saying? When one door closes, another one opens," Riley said, twirling a lock of her hair.

Chloe nodded. "Yeah. We'll make the most of Christmas in California. I'll bake cookies. We'll decorate a tree." She grinned. "You can get Christmas trees online, right?"

"Ha-ha," Riley cracked.

"By the time we're finished with Chez Dad, his trailer will look like a winter wonderland," Chloe declared.

"That's the spirit!" Riley grinned.

"You girls have your usual room," Jake Carlson said. "Just make yourselves at home."

Chloe glanced around. The trailer looked even more cluttered than usual—their dad called it "lived-in." Piles of magazines and books about spirituality littered the floor. A black yoga mat and a couple of damp beach towels were draped over the back of the futon couch. A bowl of soggy, half-eaten granola sat on the coffee table. The air was filled with the sweet, heavy smell of patchouli incense.

Chloe and Riley's mother had just dropped them off at their father's trailer on her way to the airport. Along with their suitcases and shopping bags full of gifts, Chloe had an extra bag filled with Christmas decorations and Christmas cookie ingredients.

"So, Dad!" Chloe said, trying to sound cheerful. "We're going to have Christmas together! Just the three of us!"

"Just like the old days," Riley added. "Well, minus Mom, that is."

Jake sat down on the couch, cross-legged. His feet were bare, revealing toenails that could definitely use a pedicure.

so little time

"Those were the days," he said wistfully. "Remember that Christmas when I gave your mother those pearl earrings—hidden in raw oysters on the half shell?" He laughed.

"She almost swallowed an earring," Chloe recalled. "I think one of us ended up performing the Heimlich maneuver on her."

"Dad, remember when you and Chloe tried to make a traditional roast goose?" Riley giggled. "I think you set the oven on fire."

"Fortunately the Chinese take-out place was open that day," Jake said. "That was one of the best Christmases of my life." He sighed.

"Because we burned the goose?" Chloe asked, confused.

"No," their father said with a laugh. "Because it was a real family Christmas, burned goose and all."

Outside the trailer the surf crashed against the jetties of rocks. Seagulls shrieked. No snow was falling, no carolers singing, no Yule log crackling in the fireplace.

[Chloe: This feels like anything but the white Christmas I was looking forward to. Well, that's about to change.]

Chloe stood up and rubbed her hands together. "Okay, who's going to help me decorate?" she said cheerfully.

"Decorate? What do you mean, decorate?" Jake asked her.

"I'm going to put up Christmas decorations, of course," Chloe replied. "Are you in?"

"Christmas decorations. Great idea," Jake said. He smiled at Chloe. "I'm in. Riley?"

"Just call me Riley the Reindeer," Riley said. She held two sticks of incense to her head, like antlers. Chloe and their father burst out laughing.

Soon the three Carlsons were covering the inside of the trailer with the Christmas decorations Chloe had brought. Riley hung icicle lights along the edges of the low ceiling. Chloe squeezed past her sister to drape bright silver tinsel from the linoleum counters. Then she placed red and green candles and goofy snow globes on any empty surface she could find. Their father hung a wreath made of bay leaves and berries over the small front door.

"I don't even recognize this place," Jake said, standing in the middle of the living room. "Girls, you're a couple of miracle workers!"

"You haven't seen anything yet, Dad. This weekend I'm going to find the perfect Christmas tree!" Chloe told him.

"Maybe we could put it over there," Riley said, pointing to a corner of the living room next to a small chair. "We'd have to move your Buddhist minishrine and your Elvis record collection, Dad."

"No problem," Jake said. "Although *out there* might be better." He pointed toward the open doorway and the small deck outside the trailer. "What do you think?"

While Riley and Jake continued to debate the placement of the Christmas tree, Chloe hung a few more strands of tinsel from the kitchen counter.

A pile of notes and envelopes cluttered one section of the counter. Chloe picked them up to move them out of the way.

Then something caught her eye. At the top of the pile was a small note in her father's familiar, scrawly handwriting:

> Dec. 17
> Meet Macy
> 8 P.M.
> 225 Pine Blvd

[Chloe: Huh? Why did Dad and Mom get together on December 17? Hey! I remember that night. Riley and I were home watching Buffy reruns on TV. Mom went out, wearing her killer black cocktail dress that makes her look like Demi Moore. I thought she was having a big night on the town with a client. I didn't know it was a big night on the town with Dad! What's up with that?]

"Psst!" Chloe hissed at Riley. "Over here!"

Riley frowned at Chloe. "Uh, sure. Be back in a sec, Dad."

"No problem, honey. I need to do some centering anyway. I'll be out on the deck doing my *prana* breathing exercises," Jake said.

Riley walked over to Chloe. "What is it?" she asked.

Chloe showed her the note.

Riley read it once, then twice. She didn't seem particularly impressed. "Dad had an appointment with Mom. So?"

"*So*, it was the *seventeenth*. That was the night Mom wore that black dress with the superplungey back. Remember?"

Riley shrugged. "Maybe she had a holiday party to go to afterward."

"Maybe. But what if she was wearing that dress for *Dad*?" Chloe said.

Riley chuckled. "What are you saying? That Mom and Dad were, like, on a *date*? No way."

"I'm not saying anything. I'm just saying this is kind of strange," Chloe replied.

"I think you're imagining things," Riley told her. "Now help me move Dad's dusty old records."

"Okay," Chloe said, reluctant to let go of the topic. As she followed Riley into the living room, she still couldn't help but wonder.

Was something mysterious going on between their parents?

chapter
three

"**H**ow do you keep your balance on this thing?" Charlie cried out.

Riley giggled as Charlie tried to stand up on his surfboard. He looked so . . . adorable.

"Bend your knees more!" Riley called to him as she paddled nearby, belly down, on her board. "Shift your weight with the movement of the water!"

"Okay!"

Following her instructions, Charlie finally managed to stand up. "Hey!" he yelled. "This is excellent. Now what do I do?"

"Just ride it," Riley replied. "And smile!"

"I'm smiling!"

Riley laughed. Could it get any better than this, she wondered. The sun was shining. The sky was blue. The surf at the beach was awesome. And she was with her favorite guy in the whole wide world. It was a perfect day.

Charlie had been superpsyched when he found out that Riley would be around for Christmas vacation, even though he also felt bad for her that her big Vail trip was off. He had agreed to let Riley teach him how to surf, starting this morning. He had even borrowed a board from one of his buds.

"Any excuse to spend more time with you," he'd said, giving her a kiss. "If I wipe out and hurt myself, though, you have to promise to nurse me back to health."

"Hey, I'll be right there with the first aid kit and your favorite cookies," Riley had joked.

Riley watched as Charlie rode his first wave toward shore. "Whoo-hooo!" he crowed, holding his arms out in a T position and wobbling only slightly. "Hang five!"

"That's 'hang ten'!" Riley shouted.

"Whatever!"

Charlie glided onto the beach and jumped exuberantly off his board. Riley paddled toward him. "Ready for another ride?" she called out.

"Bring it on! Hey, did I mention how cute you look in that red bikini?" Charlie said, smiling.

"Yeah, about twenty times."

"Oh. Well, make it twenty-one."

Riley blushed. Only Charlie could make her feel this way: shy and happy and nervous and excited, all at the same time.

The two of them paddled together out to the edge

of the surf. "There's a big wave coming in," Riley said, peering out at the water. "Maybe we should wait this one out."

"It's not *that* big," Charlie said. "Come on, I can handle it. Or are you scared?" he teased.

"Not me," Riley said. "But if you want to bail at the last minute, just bail, all right?"

"Yes, coach."

Floating on her board, feeling the salty spray on her face, Riley watched the wave roll in and gather steam. It *was* going to be a big one. For a second she contem-plated just *ordering* Charlie to wait it out. But she knew how stubborn he could be. Once he made up his mind about something, he wasn't likely to back down.

It was time. "Okay. Now! Start paddling toward shore!" Riley yelled.

"Got it!"

Riley and Charlie began paddling. "Stand up!" she shouted.

Riley transitioned quickly to a standing position. Her board trembled and almost buckled beneath her. She shifted her weight one way, then the other, trying to catch the rhythm of the wave.

She glanced out of the corner of her eye at Charlie. He seemed to be struggling to get up on his feet. "How are you doing?" she shouted.

"Fine! I'm almost there! I just have to— W*hoa*!"

The crest of the wave caught Charlie by surprise.

His board slid out from under him, and he tumbled into the water. The wave crashed down over his head.

"Charlie!" Riley screamed.

Ice bag. Check. Homemade macadamia-nut-chocolate-chip cookies. Check. The latest issue of *Guitar Weekly*. Check.

Riley went through the contents of her backpack, making sure she had everything. Then she parked her bike in front of Charlie's house and walked up to the front door. A small black cat was sitting on the porch. It skittered away when it saw her.

Riley still couldn't shake the guilt she'd been feeling since Charlie's accident that morning. He had wiped out on the big wave, and his right foot landed hard on a rock underwater.

He'd limped onto shore with Riley's help and called his father on her cell phone. His father drove right over. After dropping Riley off at her house, Charlie's father took him to a doctor.

Later, Charlie had called Riley and told her that he had a bad sprain. "At least it's not broken," he'd said, trying to sound brave.

Riley had decided to visit him with a care package. But now that she was at his house, she was nervous. Would he be happy to see her? What if he was mad at her about the accident? What if he blamed her for his sprained ankle?

Taking a deep breath, Riley knocked on the door.

"I'll get it!" she heard a woman's voice call from inside.

"I've got it, Mom!" came Charlie's voice in reply.

After a moment the door opened. Charlie was standing there. On crutches.

Riley's heart melted at sight of him on crutches, his ankle wrapped up in an elastic bandage. "Oh, Charlie—" she began.

"Riley!" Charlie cried out. He looked really startled. He pulled the door partly shut behind him.

Riley frowned. Why did he seem unhappy to see her? "I am so sorry about what happened," she went on. "I brought you some things to cheer you up."

"Oh!" Charlie continued to just stand there with a weird expression on his face.

"Could I come in?" Riley asked him.

"Uh . . . that's really sweet, Riley, but the doctor told me I shouldn't have any company," Charlie said, glancing over his shoulder. "She said I really needed to, uh, rest. Maybe another time?"

In the background Riley could hear two female voices talking, then breaking into laughter. "Is that your mom and sister?" she asked Charlie.

"Uh, yeah. Anyway, I really, really need to rest. I'll call you, okay?"

"Wait! Your stuff!" Riley exclaimed. She dug through her backpack and handed him the cookies, the ice bag, and the magazine.

He took them from her hastily and set them down

on a hall table. "Thanks, Riley! I'll call you! Bye!"

He closed the door.

Riley just stood there, feeling totally confused.

What's up with Charlie? she wondered. He's definitely not acting like himself.

Chloe glanced around the dining room of Chez Sophie. It was the most beautiful restaurant she had ever been in. The décor was black and silver and super-stylish. There were huge bouquets of fresh flowers everywhere. The atmosphere was totally romantic—a perfect spot for a date. Even though, in her case, it was a date with her boyfriend *and* his parents.

"Are you enjoying your *escargots*, Chloe?" Lennon's mother asked her.

"Oh, they're yummy!" Chloe said. "I've never had them before. Are they some kind of seafood?" She picked another one up and popped it into her mouth. She loved the buttery, garlicky flavor.

Lennon's father smiled. "Actually, they're snails."

Chloe stopped chewing. "Snails?"

[**Chloe**: I didn't know I was eating something that slimes around in people's gardens! Would it be totally rude if I spit it out onto my plate? Quick, change the subject. It will get your mind off what you're eating.]

"It's very nice of you to bring me here for a good-bye dinner," Chloe said sweetly to Lennon's parents. "Especially since I'm not going to Vail after all."

"It's our pleasure," Lennon's mother said.

"We'll just rename it," Lennon's father said, his eyes twinkling. "Instead of calling it a good-bye dinner, we'll call it a holiday celebration dinner with our son and his lovely girlfriend."

Chloe smiled shyly at Lennon. He was staring at his lap, his cheeks bright red. Chloe thought he looked really gorgeous in his navy-blue suit, crisp white shirt, and purple tie. She was glad she had decided to wear one of her dressiest dresses: black silk with spaghetti straps.

"This place is definitely nicer than the Newsstand," Chloe joked to Lennon. The Newsstand was a café where he worked and where Chloe and all their buds hung out.

"Definitely," Lennon agreed.

The four of them continued to talk—about the holidays, about school, about the pros and cons of living in Malibu—through the rest of the lavish dinner. Riley was right; there was something really, really nice about knowing your boyfriend's parents and being included in their lives. It made the relationship seem so real. As if she and Lennon were forever. It was a good feeling.

The waiter came by and took the *escargots* plates away, making Chloe breathe a sigh of relief. He and three other waiters proceeded to bring them more food, divided up into elegant courses.

Chloe had no idea that a dinner could consist of so many courses. After the *escargots* came a lobster bisque, which was a fancy lobster soup. Then there was a salad with baby greens. Then came a fish course, then a meat course, then a cheese course. Finally, when she didn't think she could eat another bite, the waiter brought a mouthwatering torte for dessert.

By the time the evening was over, Chloe was really stuffed. She hoped she could still get out of her seat and waddle out the door!

Lennon led her outside to the street as his parents took care of the check. The air was fresh and cool and smelled like the ocean.

Lennon kissed her lightly on the cheek. "I hope you had a good time," he said.

Chloe smiled up at him. "I had an awesome time. Your parents are so nice!"

"They're pretty okay, for parents," Lennon agreed.

Lennon leaned to give Chloe another kiss—this time on the lips. She moved closer to him. Her heart began to race. She hoped Lennon's parents wouldn't walk up behind them. . . .

But at the last minute something caught Chloe's eye. She drew back sharply.

"What?" Lennon asked, alarmed. "What's the matter?"

Chloe pointed to a sign in front of the restaurant. "That!" she cried out.

Lennon looked totally confused. "It says Chez Sophie. So?"

"It says, Chez Sophie, 225 *Pine Boulevard*," Chloe explained. "So this is where my mom and dad met a few nights ago!"

"Huh?" Lennon said.

Chloe didn't reply. Her mind was racing a mile a minute.

It was totally clear to her now. Mom dressed in her Demi Moore outfit. Dad dressed in . . . . whatever. The two of them having dinner at the most romantic restaurant in Malibu.

Her "separated" parents had definitely gone on a date!

chapter
four

"Charlie is so over me," Riley said unhappily.

"He is *not* over you," Chloe chided her. "He's just . . . going through some weird guy thing."

Riley sighed and took a bite of her wheat-free, gluten-free English muffin. It was the only breakfast food she'd found in her father's refrigerator that seemed vaguely edible. Her other choices were soy flakes or a blue-green algae shake.

It was Saturday morning. Chloe had gone on her big dinner date with Lennon and his parents last night. Riley, on the other hand, had not heard from *her* boyfriend since her less-than-successful visit to his house yesterday. She was still waiting for Charlie to call. Which he hadn't done.

"He's probably just embarrassed by his wipeout," Chloe reassured Riley. "Guys are like that."

"Maybe he blames me for the accident," Riley said. "It was my idea to give him surfing lessons."

29

"So? He's the one who insisted on riding that big wave. You tried to talk him out of it, remember?" Chloe reminded her.

Riley frowned. "Yeah. I guess. But why wouldn't he let me into his house yesterday? He practically slammed the door in my face. Does he not want me to meet his mom and sister? Is he ashamed of me?"

Chloe sighed. "I'm sure he did *not* practically slam the door in your face. He is definitely *not* ashamed of you. Look. Why don't you just call him? Just be super-casual, ask him how he's feeling."

"He should be calling me," Riley insisted. "He said he would."

"Earth to Riley. This is the twenty-first century. It's not cool to wait for your boyfriend to call you," Chloe told her.

Riley thought about that. Chloe was right. What was she doing, moping by the phone like a lovesick teenager? Of course, she *was* a lovesick teenager. But she didn't have to act that way.

Riley picked up the phone and punched in Charlie's number.

He answered after a few rings. "Hello?"

"Hey, it's me," Riley said.

"Riley! Hi!" Charlie sounded happy to hear from her. "How's it going? Hey, awesome cookies. Thanks."

Yes! Riley thought, giving Chloe a thumbs-up sign.

"I'm glad you liked them. How's your ankle feeling?"

"A little better. My mom's been making me keep it elevated."

"That's smart."

Out of the corner of her eye Riley saw Chloe scribbling something on a piece of paper. Chloe passed the paper to Riley.

It read:

Offer to go to his house tonight with his fave pizza and DVD. He can't say no to that!

Riley gave Chloe another thumbs-up sign. Her sister was brilliant! Must be the Carlson genes, she thought.

"Hey, Charlie," Riley said. "Are you busy tonight? I could come over to your house with an everything pizza. And I could bring over that new DVD with the Crash's concert clips." The Crash was one of Charlie's favorite bands.

"That sounds like fun," Charlie said.

Yea! Riley thought. Chloe was right. No way he'd say no.

"But Frodo's coming over tonight," Charlie added. "Maybe we could make it another time?"

Riley's heart sank. Frodo was one of Charlie's best buds. "Oh. Well, okay, maybe another time. Have fun with Frodo."

31

They talked for a few more minutes, then said good-bye. Riley turned to Chloe. "He's hanging out with Frodo," she explained.

"Oh," Chloe said. "Well, at least you tried. Call him tomorrow and repeat the offer. I guarantee—you *will* get inside his house. You *will* meet his mom and sister."

"Maybe," Riley said.

Chloe took a bite of Riley's organic English muffin. "Yuck! Hey, listen. I have news about Mom and Dad! Remember that piece of paper with the address on it? *Well* . . ."

Chloe went on about a romantic restaurant on Pine Boulevard with snails on the menu. Snails? But Riley was only half listening. All she could think about was Charlie.

Every time she asked to come to his house and maybe meet the rest of his family, he had an excuse.

Was it just a series of coincidences and bad timing? Or did he really want to keep the relationship status quo and not let her any deeper into his life?

"I can't believe you found such a perfect Christmas tree, Chloe," Jake said.

Chloe grinned as she draped a string of popcorn and cranberries on the tree. "Hey, I can find *anything* if I put my mind to it. Besides, it's not a real Christmas without a real Christmas tree!"

Chloe didn't tell her father how many stores she'd gone to before finding the perfect fresh evergreen tree. She also didn't mention the price tag. It was Christmas, after all!

It was Saturday night, and she and her father were decorating the tree with homemade ornaments and other decorations Chloe had dug up at the Malibu beach house. Riley was at the mall, doing some last-minute Christmas shopping with her best friend, Sierra, who'd managed to tear herself away from all her visiting relatives. Riley had said she would try to be home in time to put the star on top of the tree.

Chloe loved having some private time with her father and enjoying a holiday activity with him. But she relished this private time for another reason, too. She needed some information from him.

"So, Dad," she said innocently, "Mom said the two of you had a great time at Chez Sophie the other night."

Chloe waited, wondering if her father would rise to the bait and respond to her tiny little white lie.

"Chez Sophie?" Jake repeated. He sounded confused. "Oh, yes, the French place. Yes, that was a special evening. It's important to celebrate anniversaries."

Anniversaries? Chloe's ears perked up. Did he say anniversaries? Except she didn't remember her parents' wedding anniversary being in December.

33

Maybe they had celebrated another anniversary, like the anniversary of their first date. But, no . . . their first date had been on Valentine's Day.

"Do you think you'll be doing it again soon?" Chloe asked her father, wondering if he planned to ask her mom out again. "You know . . . making a regular thing out of it?" she added pointedly.

"Well, sure, why not?" Jake replied matter-of-factly. He pulled an ornament out of the shopping bag. "Look at this," he said, a smile spreading across his face. "Your mother and I bought this to commemorate your and Riley's first Christmas."

Chloe peered at the ornament. It was two pairs of silver baby shoes tied together with a red ribbon.

"That is so cute," Chloe said.

Her father didn't reply. He had a faraway look in his eyes, as though he were enjoying some long-ago memory.

Chloe turned back to the tree, her thoughts racing. She was now ninety percent sure her parents were dating again—or at least contemplating it. But she still needed proof.

The second her father left the trailer for his meditation class, Chloe whipped out her cell.

"Lennon? Hey, it's me. Can you meet me at Dad's trailer? I'll explain when you get here. Bye!"

● ● ●

Riley and her best friend Sierra stood on one of the longest lines Riley had ever seen, waiting to purchase—of all things—batteries. They were at the mall, doing some extremely last-minute Christmas shopping. Sierra had managed to steal away from her house full of relatives for a few hours, with a promise to buy gifts for her little cousins while she was at the mall.

"I don't think we've moved in ten minutes," Riley said with a sigh. She peered over the heads on line in front of her at the electronics shop and counted. "We're still eleventh in line. What could be taking so long up there?"

Sierra shrugged. "I don't know, but all I need are these batteries," she said in frustration. "They should have a 'batteries only' line or something."

Sierra moved her heavy shopping bags from one shoulder to the other and groaned. "I should have checked the toy boxes *before* I bought them for my cousins," she said. "Who knew such little toys would need so many batteries?"

Riley laughed. It *was* kind of annoying, standing on this crazy-long line, but it also gave her the chance to talk to Sierra, whom she hadn't seen much since the holiday vacation started. Sierra had about a million relatives visiting for the holidays, and had been held prisoner in her house for days. Worst of all, she told Riley, she'd been forced to wear all her "un-cool clothes" the whole time.

[Riley: Let me explain. Sierra's parents are great people . . . but pretty old-fashioned.

35

Sierra hates the conservative clothes they want her to wear. So she secretly changes her outfit every time she leaves her house! It's like she leads a double life most of the time.]

Tonight, Riley noticed, was an exception. Since they'd decided to meet at the mall on a whim, Sierra hadn't had time to bring a change of clothes. So she was dressed in a long skirt and a button-down shirt. Riley smiled to herself as she looked over Sierra's outfit. So *not* Sierra-like!

"So anyway," Riley said, when she noticed the line still wasn't going anywhere, "Charlie's been acting so strange since the other day, when he hurt his leg surfing. It was like he didn't want to talk to me or see me. And it occurred to me that he *never* asks me over to his house. So I went over there to give him a care package, and he practically slammed the door in my face! I'm really freaking out about this whole not-wanting-me-to-come over thing."

Sierra made a face. "Yeah, that is weird. But maybe he's embarrassed about wiping out the other day," she offered.

Riley grinned. "That's what Chloe thought, too!" she replied. Funny how her best friend and her sister were so much alike.

"He finally called and we sort of straightened things out," Riley went on. "I was even *almost* going to go over his house tonight, but he'd already made plans. His friend Frodo was going over to hang."

Just then, the line they were on moved up slightly. "Finally!" Sierra exclaimed. "Only ten more people ahead of us now!" she said happily. She readjusted her shopping bags. "Never again! Never again will I go Christmas shopping at the last minute!" she proclaimed.

"You got that right!" Riley replied. "Or maybe you should just stock up on batteries for next—" She stopped talking in mid-sentence as she stared at the customer who had just finished paying and was walking past them, out of the store.

"*Omigosh*!" Riley exclaimed. A sick feeling washed over her.

"Riley? What is it?" Sierra asked in alarm. "Are you okay?"

Riley pointed to the long-haired guy in a black T-shirt and blue jeans who was bogged down with shopping bags.

"There's *Frodo*!" she said.

Sierra's eyes widened. "Charlie's friend?" she asked.

Riley nodded as that sick feeling settled in her stomach. "Yeah," she said sadly. "The same Frodo who was *supposed* to be hanging out at Charlie's house tonight."

Riley turned to Sierra. "I can't believe this," she said, her voice choking up. "Charlie lied to me!"

"What are we looking for, exactly?" Lennon whispered to Chloe.

"You don't have to whisper, Lennon. Dad's out. He went to a meditation class," Chloe replied.

"Oh! Okay. So what are we looking for, exactly?" Lennon repeated in a loud voice.

Chloe had called Lennon as soon as her father left for the evening and asked him to come over ASAP. Ordinarily her sister would be her assistant in any and all snooping and spying matters. But Riley was still at the mall with Sierra, and, besides, she was preoccupied with her Charlie dilemma.

Riley had just called from the mall on her cell and reported a piece of bad news. She'd run into Frodo, Charlie's bud. After exchanging some small talk, Riley had figured out that Frodo did not have plans with Charlie for that night, which was what Charlie told Riley. Charlie had lied to her. But why? Chloe hated to admit it, but things weren't looking so great for her sister and Charlie.

"Just look for anything dated December seventeenth of this year," Chloe instructed Lennon. "Also, look for anything that might be a clue to my mom and dad's relationship."

"So you really think they're dating again?" Lennon asked her.

"Yeah, or *almost* dating again. I'm not sure," Chloe replied.

The two of them began searching the trailer in earnest. Lennon had never really seen the inside of it before.

"What is *this*?" Lennon asked, picking up a jar full of dried plants and other mysterious substances. "It looks really nasty."

"That's Dad's Chinese tea mixture," Chloe replied. "It's, like, medicine. It has a bunch of weird stuff in it, like dried herbs and bugs."

"Bugs? That *is* nasty," Lennon observed.

"Yeah. But who are we to talk? We ate snails last night," Chloe reminded him with a giggle.

"True." Lennon laughed.

The two of them proceeded to search the trailer. After a while Lennon glanced up from the folding table Jake used as a desk. It was missing a leg, so it was propped up with an old tennis racket. "I found something!" Lennon announced.

"What?" Chloe cried out. She rushed over to join him, almost tripping on a pile of laundry as she did so.

Lennon pointed to a small white piece of paper. It was a receipt from the Black Iris—a florist—dated December 17!

Chloe gasped. This was huge!

"Dad bought Mom flowers on December seventeenth," she said. "This *definitely* means they were on a romantic date that night!"

chapter
five

Riley stepped over Chloe to grab a roll of silver wrapping paper. Her leg accidentally knocked into Chloe's arm, causing Chloe to drop the box she'd been wrapping.

"Oh, sorry!" Riley apologized.

"No problem. Battlefield conditions." Chloe grinned at her sister.

It was Christmas Eve. Riley and Chloe were doing some last-minute wrapping in the tiny bedroom in their father's trailer. Wrapping paper, gift boxes, and ribbons covered every inch of floor space in the cramped room.

"You're not kidding!" Riley chuckled. "This is definitely not like Christmas at our mom's house."

"You're not kidding," Chloe repeated.

Still, Riley had to admit that she and Chloe had made things pretty Christmas-y in their father's trailer. They had put up an awesome tree with all kinds of

reached over and picked up the cordless phone on the table beside her.

"Hello?"

"Hey, Riley? It's me."

Riley's heart skipped a beat. It was Charlie!

"Hey," she said happily. "How are you?"

"Pretty good. Merry Christmas!"

"Merry Christmas!"

"I miss you," he added.

He misses me! Riley thought. Maybe this space thing does work after all?

"I miss you, too," she said, meaning it. "How was your Christmas?"

"Not bad," Charlie said. "I got a new DVD player for my room."

"Excellent! And how's your ankle?"

"Better. Listen, do you want to get together and do something today? I want to give you your Christmas present."

"I want to give you your Christmas present, too," Riley told him. "But what about your ankle?"

"It's cool. I'm off the crutches, and I can get around as long as I take it easy. I could come over, and we could hang out on the beach or something."

"Sounds great," Riley agreed.

After they decided on a time, Riley said good-bye and hung up. She leaned back in the beach chair and glanced up at the sky again. There wasn't a single cloud in sight.

The day after Christmas was suddenly looking up, she thought with a happy grin. *Way* up.

"I hope you like it," Charlie said.

Smiling shyly, he handed Riley a small box wrapped in pink and silver paper.

She and Charlie were hanging out on the beach near her father's trailer. They were completely alone except for an occasional jogger or two and a family of seagulls.

Riley smiled back at Charlie. Sitting on a beach blanket with him, holding hands, she could almost forget about their last weird encounter at his house—as well as the fact that he had lied to her about having plans with Frodo.

She knew she had to ask him why he had lied to her. But right now she was having such a good time with him that she didn't want to break the spell.

She looked down at the pink and silver package. "What is it?" she asked him, curious.

Charlie chuckled. "Open it and find out. And don't shake it—that's cheating!" he teased her.

"I won't." Riley giggled.

She unwrapped the pretty paper and opened the white box. Inside was a purple leather choker with the initial R on it in silver.

"Wow!" Riley cried out. She lifted the choker out of the box and held it up. Sunlight winked off the perfectly shaped silver R. "It's beautiful!"

"Do you like it, really?" Charlie asked her.

"I love it! Thank you!" Riley leaned over and kissed him on the cheek.

"I'm glad you like it," Charlie said, kissing her, too. "Okay, now where's my present?" he joked.

He shifted his weight slightly and rubbed his ankle. It was still wrapped in an elastic bandage.

"Are you okay?" Riley asked him, concerned.

"Yeah. Just a little sore," Charlie replied.

"Are you in pain? Do you want to go home?"

"Definitely not. I want my present now!" Charlie laughed.

Riley reached into her backpack and pulled out the blue box. "Here," she said, handing it to him. "I hope you don't have it already."

Charlie tore open the wrapping. "The latest Crash CD!" he crowed. "Excellent! I've been dying to get this one!"

"I haven't heard it yet. Maybe we could listen to it together," Riley suggested.

"Totally," Charlie agreed.

He leaned over and gave her a thank-you kiss. His lips grazed hers lightly, then lingered there. They kissed for a long time.

Riley was confused. But she was happy, too. For the moment she forgot about the fact that Charlie was keeping her at arm's length from his house and his family. She was *in* his arms here and now. Everything was fine between them again.

Chloe did one last search of the trailer to make sure no one was home. She felt kind of silly doing it. The trailer was so tiny, she would be able to tell in two seconds if she wasn't alone. Besides, she knew for a fact that Riley was out giving their dad a surfing lesson until dinnertime. But she *had* to make sure.

"Okay, Carlson, coast is clear," she told herself.

She went into the bedroom she shared with Riley, pushed aside a pile of just-laundered towels, and pulled her laptop computer out from its hiding place. She booted it up and signed on to her e-mail account. Or, rather, Jake246's e-mail account.

The mailman icon was blinking. "You have three new messages!" the computerized voice cried out.

"Yes!" Chloe said, pumping a fist in the air. Her mother must have responded to her father's e-mail—three times!

But when Chloe saw the first two messages, she realized they were just spam. The subject heading on the first message read: BECOME A MILLIONAIRE IN JUST 10 DAYS! Yeah, right, Chloe thought. She hit the DELETE button.

The subject heading of the second e-mail was similar: LOSE 30 POUNDS ON THE CARROT JUICE DIET! Chloe hit the DELETE button again.

But Chloe struck gold with the third e-mail. It was from her mother's Blackberry e-mail address! The subject heading read: MERRY CHRISTMAS.

Chloe opened the e-mail and began to read it eagerly.

```
Dear Jake: I'm glad you and the girls
had a good Christmas. Really wish I
could have been there. Rose is doing
better. Favor—could you stop by the
house and check to make sure that the
A/C in the living room is off? Also,
plz check to see if family health
insurance premium is due on 12/31.
See you soon.
Thnx, Macy
```

Chloe read the message a second time, then a third. She frowned. Her mother's e-mail was so businesslike. Of course, that was typical Macy Carlson. Still, couldn't she have given Jake246 *something*?

She did write *Dear Jake*, Chloe thought. She could have written *Hi, Jake, Good afternoon, Jake,* or just, *Jake*. But *Dear Jake*—that was personal, intimate. Her mother wasn't one to reveal her feelings directly. Maybe *Dear Jake* was her *indirect* way of expressing her emotions for her estranged husband?

And what about that *Really wish I could have been there* business? What did *that* mean? Was Macy indicating that she wished she could have been in Malibu with the whole family? Or with Jake in particular? And what about that *really* part? That seemed pretty mushy, in Chloe's opinion.

Chloe hit the REPLY key and started composing an e-mail from Jake246 to Macy.

```
Dear Macy: I'm so glad to hear from
you! Listen, I was thinking. I had a
great time at Chez Sophie with you.
When you get back, what do you say we
go back there again and relive the
magic of December 17? I promise you
that
```

Just then Chloe heard the front door open.

"Hello?" a female voice called out.

Chloe was startled. She thought Riley was still out surfing with their father.

"Riley? I'm in here!" Chloe shouted.

A minute later the door to the tiny bedroom opened.

But it wasn't Riley.

It was Mom!

chapter
seven

"**M**om!" Chloe cried out. "What are *you* doing here?"

Macy laughed. "What kind of welcome is *that*?" she demanded, putting down her suitcase.

Chloe quickly pushed a button to activate her screen saver. A version of "Jingle Bells" meowed by cats began blasting from her computer's speakers. Nope, wrong button. She pushed another one. The screen filled up with a picture of her and Lennon at the fair, sharing an ice cream cone. Whew!

"Chloe, you're acting very strangely," Macy remarked. "Am I interrupting some romantic chat session with Lennon or something?"

Chloe's heart was pounding. Her mother had almost caught her composing an e-mail to her from Jake246!

"Nope!" Chloe said. "You just surprised me, that's

all. What are you doing back so early?" She jumped up and gave her mother a big hug.

"Douglas flew in from Australia late last night to take care of Aunt Rose. So I took the first flight I could get out of Portland," Macy explained. She glanced around. "Where is everybody?"

"You mean, where's Dad?" Chloe said with a knowing smile.

Macy frowned at her. She looked puzzled. "I meant Riley *and* your father. Where are they?"

Just then Chloe heard the front door open—then a peal of laughter. "You should have seen yourself when you were about to get pounded by that killer wave!" Chloe heard Riley say.

Macy rushed out to the living room. Chloe followed right behind her.

Riley and their dad were standing in the doorway.

"Mom!" Riley cried out. She set down her surfboard.

"Macy!" Jake cried out at the same time. He was wearing his Hawaiian floral-print swim shorts. He was also dripping wet.

"Surprise!" Macy exclaimed, throwing her arms up in the air.

"Macy! What are you doing here?" Jake said happily. "We weren't expecting you for days."

"Great-aunt Rose's son Douglas came home early. I wanted to surprise you guys." Macy grinned.

Jake rushed up to her and clasped her in a big bear hug, effectively soaking her jacket front. She didn't seem to mind, Chloe noted happily.

"This is just great. Isn't it great, girls?" Jake asked.

"Yeah, Dad, it's great," Chloe said.

Chloe looked at Riley. Riley smiled. It was pretty obvious to both of them. Their parents seemed glad to see each other. *Very* glad.

After a moment Riley gave her mother a hug, too. "I was just giving Dad a surfing lesson," she explained.

Macy raised her eyebrows. "Oh? How did it go?"

"Yeah, Dad, you look kind of banged up," Chloe said. He had some nasty-looking bruises on his arms and legs.

Jake waved a hand dismissively. "These? They're just battle scars. I mastered those waves. I rode the big kahunas. I hung ten. It was, uh, fat!" He waggled his eyebrows at Macy.

Macy laughed. Jake laughed, too.

[Chloe: There's no doubt about it. Dad is trying really hard to impress Mom. And some major sparks are definitely flying between them!]

Riley popped a handful of potato chips into her mouth. "So," she said to Chloe. "I think Project Mom and Dad is going really well."

The potato chips tasted sandy. Riley grimaced and downed them with a long swig of soda. She and

Chloe had been so eager to take a snack break after their long surfing session that she had forgotten to rinse the sand off her hands.

Chloe leaned back on their beach blanket. "I think it's going well, too," she agreed. "Mom's coming home yesterday changed things a little, though. We might have to adjust our strategy."

"Are you still planning on doing the romantic New- Year's-Eve thing?" Riley asked her.

Chloe nodded. "Uh-huh. A dozen red roses, champagne, the works. I talked to Manuelo before he left on his vacation, and he set aside a bottle of super-fancy champagne for the occasion. He hid it in the veggie bin of the fridge. Mom *never* looks in there." Manuelo was the Carlsons' trusty housekeeper and friend. "I just have to figure out a menu," Chloe added.

"I can help with that," Riley offered. "Dad likes vegetarian-health-food anything. Mom likes the opposite—filet mignon, lobster, and lots of rich, creamy sauces. No problem," she joked.

Chloe giggled. "We'll figure out something. In the meantime we don't have to send Mom fake e-mails from Dad anymore. We can help speed their relationship along in person!"

"What do you mean?" Riley asked her. She broke a potato chip in half and tossed the pieces to a seagull that was lingering near the beach blanket. It scooped a chip up in its beak and flew away.

"Like, we can arrange for them to accidentally run into each other in dark, cozy places," Chloe explained. "Stuff like that."

"Brilliant!" Riley said enthusiastically.

Chloe nodded. "By the time New Year's Eve rolls around, they'll be ready for romance!"

"Definitely," Riley agreed.

Chloe leaned forward. "Speaking of romance . . . how are things going with Charlie?"

Riley smiled. She fingered the purple choker with the silver R. She hadn't taken it off since he gave it to her.

"Everything's back to normal," she told Chloe happily. "He came over yesterday, and we hung out on the beach. He was his old self again. He gave me this totally amazing necklace, and then he kissed me, and—" She broke off, blushing.

Chloe gave Riley a hug. "I'm so glad for you! Didn't I tell you it would work out? Guys are funny. Sometimes they go through this bizarre emotional-disconnect thing. But then they come back."

"Whatever it was, I'm glad he's back," Riley said. "Speaking of which, do you mind if we swing by his house on our way home? It's, like, two blocks away. I want to say hi."

"No problem. We can say hey to your sweetie bear." Chloe giggled.

Sweetie bear? Riley thought. Where does she come up with this stuff?

Riley and Chloe took a couple more rides while the waves were still good. Then they packed up their things, pulled their shorts on over their bathing suits, and headed for Charlie's house.

When they got there, Riley turned to Chloe. "I have a good feeling about this. After our date on the beach yesterday, I think he's finally going to ask me inside! And maybe even introduce me to his mom and sister!"

"Do you want me to take off?" Chloe offered. "Maybe this should be a private boyfriend-girlfriend moment."

Riley shook her head. "No way! I want you by my side. It would be cool for you to meet his family, too."

Chloe grinned. "Whatever you say. Lead the way."

They walked up to the front door. Riley rang the bell.

"I'll get it, Mom!" came Charlie's voice from inside. The door opened. Charlie stood there, smiling. Then his smile faded. "Riley!" he gasped.

Uh-oh, Riley thought. He's got that panicked look again.

"I mean, hey, Riley," Charlie said. He gave a little cough. "Hey, Chloe. Listen, I've got a terrible case of the, um, flu. Yeah." He gave another cough, a louder one this time. "You guys shouldn't be here. I'm really contagious!"

"But, Charlie—" Riley said.

60

"Really, *really* contagious. So you'd better go. I'll give you a call!" Charlie said. He closed the door.

Riley couldn't believe it. She didn't know whether to cry or scream.

She turned to Chloe. "He totally does not have the flu," she said quietly.

Chloe opened her mouth. Riley could tell she was about to try to give the whole thing a positive spin.

"He totally does *not* have the flu," Riley repeated firmly.

Chloe clamped her mouth shut. After a second she said, "You're right."

"I guess I was wrong before," Riley said angrily. "Thing aren't back to normal between Charlie and me after all!"

chapter
eight

"I believe this is the last of your stuff," Jake Carlson said, setting Chloe and Riley's suitcases down in the front hall of the beach house.

"Thanks, Dad!" Chloe said, hugging him. "You're the best!"

"Yeah, we had an awesome Christmas with you," Riley agreed.

Chloe noticed that Riley looked a little down. She knew her sister was still bummed about their surprise visit to Charlie's house earlier that day.

Now that their mother was home, Chloe and Riley were moving back to their usual house. Their dad had driven them there, along with all their suitcases and Christmas presents.

Their mom was in the kitchen, speaking to one of her clients on the phone. Chloe could hear her rattling off names, dates, and figures in her breathless, mile-a-minute business voice: "No, we rescheduled that meeting from Monday to Thursday because Monday overlaps with the Loca Loco fall line press conference. Yes, *Vogue* is sending somebody." Her mother never stopped working!

"I'll just say good-bye to your mother, and then I'll be going," their father said. He pulled a gray peace-logo sweatshirt over his head. "I'm sure you three have a lot of catching up to do."

Was it her imagination, or did Chloe hear a hint of wistful longing in her father's voice? "Dad, what are you doing for dinner?" she asked him on impulse.

Jake shrugged. "Nothing exciting. I think I've got some of that leftover broccoli casserole in the refrigerator."

Chloe and Riley exchanged a look. Was this an opportunity for some up-close-and-personal-time between their parents?

"Dad! Why don't you have dinner with us?" Chloe suggested.

"Yeah, why don't you?" Riley added.

"We'll have . . . uh . . . something really special," Chloe improvised. "It'll be kind of a welcome-back-Mom thing."

"What a great idea!" Jake said eagerly. "Yes. I'd love to stay for dinner. Are you sure it's going to be okay with your mom?"

"I'm sure she'd be totally thrilled if you stayed," Chloe gushed.

I hope that's true, Chloe thought, suddenly

63

worried. What if Mom *isn't* thrilled?

As soon as Macy Carlson got off the phone, Chloe intercepted her and dragged her into the living room before she had a chance to make another phone call.

"Riley and I are going to make you a welcome-home dinner, Mom," Chloe announced. "Dad's agreed to stay and help us celebrate!"

"Isn't that nice of him?" Riley piped up.

"You two just sit on the couch and, um, talk. Riley and I will be in the kitchen," Chloe said. She took their mother's hand and led her to the couch. Riley, catching on, steered their father over to the couch to sit next to their mother.

Macy frowned at Chloe and Riley. "But I have work to do, and—" she began.

"No work for an hour! Just relax and enjoy the wonderful dinner Riley and I are going to make for you," Chloe told her.

"I can't wait," Jake said.

"Wonderful dinner?" Riley whispered to Chloe as the two of them headed into the kitchen. "What wonderful dinner?"

"It's called creative microwaving," Chloe whispered back. "I'm sure Manuelo left some baggies of frozen food in the freezer."

Riley nodded. "Right. We just won't tell Mom and Dad about the 'frozen' part. Hey, I could put a salad together!"

"That's the spirit. Now, where's the fuse box . . . or the circuit breakers or whatever?" Chloe muttered.

"Fuse box? What does that have to do with cooking dinner?" Riley asked, confused.

"Not cooking dinner, silly. Notice that the sun has gone down? And that it's really dark outside? We're going to arrange a little romantic blackout for the happy couple," Chloe told her.

"Chloe, you're brilliant!" Riley praised her.

"Runs in the family." Chloe grinned.

Chloe and Riley managed to find the circuit breaker in the utility closet. Chloe studied it, frowning. There were a lot of switches with mysterious-looking letters and numbers next to them.

"Now what?" Chloe said.

"Why don't we start flipping the switches?" Riley suggested.

"All of them, or just some of them?" Chloe asked her.

Riley shrugged. "We could do them one at a time and see what happens."

"Okay. Here goes."

Chloe took a deep breath, then flipped the first switch on the top left side. Then she flipped the second one. Then the third.

Riley peered around the corner. "The light in the hallway just went off!" she whispered excitedly. "Keep going!"

Chloe continued flipping. Soon the entire house

seemed to be bathed in blackness.

"What's happening?" they heard their mom exclaim from the living room.

"I think we're having a blackout!" they heard their father reply.

Then there was the sound of breaking glass and a loud scream. It was Mom!

Chloe and Riley quickly found their way to the living room, trying not to stumble in the darkness. Chloe saw her mother sprawled on the floor. Next to her was the coffee table, overturned. A lamp, too.

"Mom? Are you okay?" Riley exclaimed.

"I—I'm fine," Macy replied in a shaky voice. "I just tripped. My head—"

"What's wrong with your head?" Chloe asked.

"She tripped and banged her head on the coffee table," Jake said worriedly. "Where does it hurt? Here?" He touched her left temple.

"Ow! Stop that!" Macy yelled at him.

"Sorry," Jake said.

"Is it bleeding?" Riley asked her anxiously.

"No, it's not bleeding. It's just a small bump. Honestly, I'm fine," Macy said.

"Girls, can you go get some candles and flashlights so we can see?" their father asked them.

"Uh, sure," Chloe said. "No problem, Dad."

Chloe felt awful. She thought she had come up with a clever scheme to create a romantic moment for her parents. But instead, the blackout was anything but romantic!

"Mission aborted," Chloe whispered to Riley as they rushed out of the living room. "I'm going to reset the circuit breakers."

"Good idea. I'll go to get Mom some ice," Riley whispered back.

Chloe headed back to the circuit breakers in the utility closet and flipped all the switches back to their original positions. After a moment all the lights came back on.

Chloe returned to the living room. "Hey, we've got power again!" she announced. "I guess the, uh, blackout's over!"

Her mother was lying on the couch with her feet up. Riley was pressing an ice bag against her head. "How does that feel, Mom?" Riley asked her.

"Like I'm going to have a monster headache for the next twenty-four hours," Macy complained.

"I have just the thing for that," Jake piped up. "I have some terrific Chinese tea at home that I could go get and brew up for you. It's the thing for headaches."

"No herbs!" Macy grumbled. "Chloe, honey, would you go down the street and get me a double latte and a big bottle of ibuprofen?"

"Caffeine and over-the-counter medications are not what you need right now," Jake told Macy firmly.

"Oh, yes, they are," Macy said, glaring at him.

"Even the latest medical journals agree that Eastern medicine can sometimes be more effective than Western medicine," Jake persisted.

"Right now the only 'medicine' I want is the kind that comes in a white plastic bottle and a Jumpin' Java cup," Macy shot back. "Now please stop lecturing me, Jake. You're making my headache worse."

Jake frowned unhappily. "Fine!"

"Fine!"

Chloe looked at Riley in alarm. "Uh, this reminds me of the time Dad dressed up in a Santa Claus costume and tripped over his own boots, and we had to take him to the ER in the middle of the night," she said brightly. "Remember that, guys? Ha-ha!"

"Ha-ha!" Riley joined in.

Their parents continued to glare at each other.

[Chloe: Okay. It would be the understatement of the year to say that the blackout plan was a huge failure. Riley and I had better come up with another plan—fast!]

It was almost eleven o'clock at night. Riley was lying in bed, staring at the cordless phone that was cradled in her lap.

She picked it up and began to dial. Then she stopped and hung up.

She had been doing this for the last half hour. Chloe had convinced her that she should call Charlie and have a major heart-to-heart with him about what had happened that afternoon, as well as all the other things that had been happening lately. Like his lie about Frodo. Like his lying about having the flu. Like his not letting her into his house or introducing her to the rest of his family.

Something was obviously up. Charlie had been playing a serious game of hot-and-cold with her. It was important that Riley get to the bottom of it.

She took a deep breath and picked up the phone again. This time she punched in his number and didn't hang up.

"Hello?" It was Charlie's voice on the other end.

Riley took another deep breath. "Hey . . . it's me," she said.

"Riley! Hey! I'm so glad you called."

Riley smiled, confused. Charlie sounded really psyched to hear from her. But just hours ago he had practically pushed her out the door, claming to have the flu. Talk about playing hot-and-cold!

"Listen, Riley," Charlie went on, "I'm really sorry about the way I acted when you and your sister came by. My ankle was acting up, and I hadn't taken a shower, so I looked like a major grunge monster, and . . ."

Just then Charlie's voice trailed off. Riley heard him laughing.

Riley frowned. What was going on? "Charlie? Are you there? Are you okay?"

Riley heard a muffled sound, as though Charlie had put a hand over the mouthpiece. "Tabatha, cut it out!" she heard him say.

Tabatha? Who was that?

"Charlie?" Riley said, confused. "Who's Tabatha? Charlie, are you there?"

There were more muffled sounds, then Charlie came back on the line. "Oh, hey," he said, sounding totally flustered.

"Who's your friend Tabatha?" Riley repeated.

"Tabatha? I don't have a friend named Tabatha," Charlie said. He laughed nervously.

Riley's heart froze. Charlie was lying to her . . . again.

And then it occurred to her. Did Charlie have another girl with him—a girl named Tabatha?

Was Charlie dating another girl? Riley wondered, getting more and more upset. That would explain a lot of things!

You creep, Riley thought angrily. You awful, two-timing creep!

She slammed the phone down as hard as she could.

chapter
nine

The walkway to the Malibu Convention Hall was lined with tall, swaying palm trees. The banner over the front entrance read, in turquoise and orange letters: WELCOME TO SURF EXPO!

"How long do we have to stay at this thing?" Macy Carlson asked, glancing at her watch. "I have a conference call at two."

Chloe laced an arm through her mother's. "Mom, get into the spirit! This is a family outing," she said. She glanced meaningfully at her father, who was walking ahead with Riley.

"Of course," Macy said with an apologetic smile. "I know how much it means to you girls. Oops! Sorry, I'm being beeped!" She grabbed her pager out of her pocket.

Chloe sighed. She hoped this expedition was going to be a success. She had thought that by having a "family outing," she could show her parents how nice it would be to be a family again. What better way to speed their newly budding relationship along?

Riley had managed to snag four tickets to the sold-out, superpopular Surf Expo. It was one of *the* events of the year. Chloe had figured that there would be something for everyone: cool surfer fashions for Mom, cool surfer culture for Dad to explore, and, of course, cool surfer *anything* for Riley and herself.

The four of them followed the crowd through the front entrance and presented their tickets at the turnstile. The guy who took their tickets was wearing nothing but a pair of blue and silver surfer shorts.

"Enjoy!" he said to the Carlsons as another guy draped fresh-flower leis over their heads.

The Carlsons started down one of the aisles, which was strewn with glistening white sand and crushed seashells. On either side of the aisle were colorful booths displaying state-of-the-art surfboards and surfing memorabilia.

A hip-hop version of "Surfin' USA" was playing over the loudspeakers. There were real potted palm trees and tropical flowers everywhere.

"This is cool," Chloe said as she took in the scenery.

"*Way* cool," Riley agreed.

Chloe glanced at her sister. She knew Riley was trying to be brave for the sake of the family—and for the sake of Project Mom and Dad. But Chloe could tell that she was still really bummed about her relationship problems with Charlie.

"Oh, look, there's Johnny Sunshine!" Jake exclaimed suddenly. He pointed to a guy standing at one of the booths. He was short and tanned with long, shiny black hair.

"Johnny Sunshine?" Chloe repeated. "Is he a folk singer or something?"

Jake chuckled. "No, honey. He's one of the world's greatest surfers. He's from Hawaii. I just read an article about him last night."

"Oh, look, there's Vanessa Sung!" Macy cried out.

"Is she a celebrity surfer, too?" Riley asked her.

Macy shook her head. "She's a designer. Surf wear, hip-hop fashions, you name it. I've been trying to hook up with her for ages. Excuse me!"

Macy made a beeline for Vanessa Sung's booth.

"Mom!" Chloe called out after her. But it was no use. Macy had shifted into full networking mode.

Jake made a face. "Same old Macy," he murmured. "She can't enjoy an afternoon out without negotiating a business deal or two."

Uh-oh, Chloe thought. This is not going the way I planned at all! Mom and Dad are supposed to be walking arm in arm, laughing, and enjoying being a family again!

"She'll be right back!" Chloe reassured him. "Come on, Dad, let's go get a pineapple-coconut smoothie!"

"As long as it's organic," Jake said. "You know how I feel about pesticides."

Chloe, Riley, and their dad walked over to the Smoothie Hut and ordered some smoothies. A short while later Macy came rushing up to their table.

Finally, Chloe thought.

"Hey, guys!" Macy said breathlessly.

"Hey, Mom, you want a smoothie?" Chloe asked her eagerly.

Macy shook her head. "Love one, but Vanessa Sung invited me to a private fashion show she's having in five. Go on and enjoy the rest of the Expo without me, 'kay? See you later!"

"I knew it," Jake said under his breath.

Macy stopped and turned on her heels. "Excuse me?"

"I said I knew you wouldn't be able to get through an entire event like this without working," Jake said with a sigh.

"Well, at least I *work*, unlike some people, who spend all their time meditating," Macy replied tersely.

"At least you two introduced each other to your families when you were first dating," Riley added miserably.

Her parents stopped arguing and stared at her. "Huh?" they said in unison.

"Never mind," Riley grumbled. She reached for her smoothie and took a long sip.

Macy glanced at her watch. "Vanessa's show is starting. I've got to run."

"Don't worry, we'll have plenty of fun without you!" Jake said, waving.

[**Chloe**: **Cut! This isn't how this scene is supposed to go!**]

"Who wants another smoothie?" Chloe said weakly.

Her mom took off. Her dad downed his smoothie. Riley looked off into space, sighing.

Chloe realized that Project Mom and Dad was going nowhere fast. No one was having a good time at the Surf Expo. It was time to get off this wave and find another one!

chapter
ten

The little mailman icon on Riley's computer screen was flashing like crazy.

YOU'VE GOT 20 MESSAGES! it read.

Twenty messages? Riley thought. She sat down at her desk and scrolled down the message list.

They were all from Charlie.

Riley, Chloe, and their mom had just gotten home from their disastrous afternoon at the Surf Expo. Mom was already working, of course. Dad had gone back to his trailer. Chloe had escaped to her room to regroup and rethink her strategy to get their parents back together.

Riley hadn't checked her e-mail since last night, when she overheard Charlie flirting with some girl named Tabatha. Her blood still boiled at the thought of it. He had been leading Riley on all this time, playing hot-and-cold with her, all the while dating some other girl in secret! How dare he?

Riley glared at the screen. All the subject headings were similar:

```
Please call
Please call ASAP
Please talk to me
Please call!!!
```

And on and on. Riley was tempted to hit the DELETE ALL button.

But she couldn't make herself do it. What the heck, she thought. She started reading his messages.

```
Dear Riley, I don't know what I did to
make you hang up on me. I know I
haven't been a great boyfriend lately.
I want to talk to you. Please call me!
Love, Charlie

Dear Riley, Please call!
Love, Charlie

Dear Riley, Please, please call me!!!
You can't ignore me forever.
Love, Charlie
```

Oh, yes, I can, Riley thought huffily.

"Riley!"

Her mother knocked briskly, then walked into Riley's room. She was carrying her cell phone in one hand and the landline phone in the other.

"You have about ten voice-mail messages on here," Macy said, handing the land-line phone to Riley.

"Ten?" said Riley.

"Yes. Can you clear them, please? *Ah, oui, bonsoir, je m'appelle* Macy Carlson *de l'Etats Unis*," Macy said into her cell phone.

"Thank you," Riley said, taking the phone from her mother, who left the room, introducing herself to someone in French.

Riley had a pretty good idea who had left her all those voice-mail messages. She dialed into the voice mail system, punched in her password, and started listening to her messages.

The first one was from Charlie. "It's me. Call me, okay?" he said.

For a second Riley's heart melted at the sound of his voice. It was so deep, so wonderful, so . . . familiar.

But the second message made her heart turn back to ice. "What did I do that was so awful?" Charlie said. "I really want you to talk to me."

I'll talk to you, all right, Riley thought angrily. She began deleting the remaining messages, since they were probably all from Charlie anyway. I'll come over and talk to you in person. And that's going to be the last conversation we ever have!

Riley rang Charlie's doorbell.

"I'll get that, Mom!" came Charlie's voice from inside.

After a moment the door opened. Charlie was standing there, wearing headphones, listening to a CD on his portable CD player.

When he saw Riley, his mouth dropped open. He tore off his headphones.

"Uh, hey, Riley," he said, glancing nervously over his shoulder. "I'm really glad to see you. But what are you doing here?"

Riley took a deep breath. *Here goes*, she thought. She tried to focus on how mad she was and not on how cute he looked in his faded teal T-shirt and denim shorts. Riley crossed her arms over her chest. "Charlie, I want to break up!" she announced.

"*What?*" Charlie gasped.

He looked really upset. For a second Riley was tempted to take back her words and give him a comforting hug. But she knew she had to do this. It was for the best.

"Why do you want to break up?" Charlie asked her, sounding hurt.

"I have, like, four good reasons," Riley told him, holding up her fingers to count. "One, you won't treat me like a real girlfriend. You refuse to let me into your house, and you won't introduce me to your mom or your sister. Real boyfriends let their girlfriends meet their families!"

"Let me explain," Charlie said quickly.

But Riley wasn't interested in any lame explanations. "Two, you lied to me about hanging out with Frodo on Saturday night," she went on. "You said I couldn't come over with pizza and a DVD because you were hanging with Frodo. But I ran into Frodo that night at the mall! And he didn't know what I was talking about!"

"Let me explain," Charlie repeated.

"Three, you were totally lying to me and Chloe the other day about having the flu. You were just trying to keep me out of your house—again!"

"Let me—"

"And four—the worst one of all—you have another girlfriend!" Riley blurted out.

"Another girlfriend?" Charlie exclaimed. He looked completely confused. "What are you talking about, Riley?"

"Don't deny it, Charlie. Her name is Tabatha. She was here with you last night when I called!" Riley accused him.

Charlie stared at her in shock. And then he broke into laughter.

Riley couldn't believe it. The two-timing jerk was *laughing* at her!

"What is so funny?" she demanded.

Still laughing, Charlie glanced over his shoulder. Then he turned and put his hands on Riley's shoulders. His expression was more serious now.

"I think it's time you came into my house," he said. "I have a *lot* of explaining to do."

"Huh?" Riley said. Now it was *her* turn to be confused.

"Just come inside. Okay?"

Riley was speechless. After all this time Charlie was finally inviting her into his house. What was going on here?

Charlie took her by the hand and led her into the living room. At least, Riley *thought* it was the living room.

Riley couldn't believe what she saw. There were at least a dozen cats in the room. Some of them were curled up, taking naps. Some of them were playing with ratty-looking cat toys. Some of them were chasing other cats.

"Rover, cut it out!" Charlie yelled at a skinny black cat that was scratching furiously at a bookshelf. Its claws had left deep gouges in the wood.

"Marmalade, leave Amanda alone!" he yelled at an orange cat that was hissing at a small calico kitten.

"Are you guys running a cat shelter?" Riley asked Charlie in amazement.

Charlie shook his head. "No, not exactly. Well, sort of. See, my mom and Tess—that's my sister—are totally obsessed with saving stray cats. They bring them home and take care of them, then try to find new owners for them."

"That's cool," Riley said. "It sounds like a really good cause."

"Maybe. But it's totally embarrassing for me to bring people into the house. I mean, look at this!" Charlie waved a hand at the snoring cats, the scratched-up furniture, and the clumps of cat hair everywhere.

"So it's not exactly something out of *Beautiful Homes* magazine," Riley said, shrugging. "Your mom and sister are doing something important. I mean, we're talking about homeless cats!"

"Yeah, I know," Charlie agreed. "But now do you understand why I didn't want you to come over? I didn't want you to think my family was a bunch of freaks. That's why I lied to you about Frodo and having the flu and stuff."

"Oh," Riley said. Now it all made sense to her. Except one thing. . . .

"But who's Tabatha?" Riley asked him.

Charlie grinned. He leaned down and picked up a fat, long-haired white and black cat that was snoozing on the couch.

"Riley, meet Tabatha. Tabatha, meet Riley," Charlie said. Tabatha opened one green eye sleepily and let out a loud meow of protest. "She was bugging me last night while I was talking on the phone with you," Charlie went on. "She jumped up onto my lap and started licking my face. That's why I told her to stop. I can't believe you thought it was another girl!"

Riley laughed and stroked Tabatha on the head. Tabatha began purring. "Now that I've met her, I can't believe it either," she admitted.

"Charles, who's this?"

Riley turned around. A tall, slender woman was standing in the living room doorway. She had curly grayish-blond hair that was pinned up loosely with lots of mismatched rhinestone pins. She had a warm, friendly face and cheerful blue eyes.

"Oh, hey, Mom. This is Riley Carlson," Charlie explained. "Riley, this is my mom."

Charlie's mother rushed over to Riley and pumped her hand up and down. "So nice to meet you, Riley! I do hope you like cats," she said merrily.

"Oh, I *love* cats," Riley told her.

"Great! Can we interest you in a couple?" Charlie's mom asked. "There's a pair of adorable calico twins that are very eager for a home, and—"

"Mom!" Charlie protested. "Riley's just visiting."

Just then a girl came trotting down the stairs. She had curly reddish-brown hair and gold wire-rimmed glasses. She looked to be about seventeen.

She was studying a clipboard. "According to my schedule, we need to give Annabelle and Dexter their ear medication," she announced. "Annabelle, left ear. Dexter, both ears."

"Tess," said Charlie.

"Plus, we need to give Pancake, Georgie, and Mittens their hair-ball-control dry food, and Petunia her vegetarian wet food—she's allergic to meat and fish—"

"Tess!" Charlie repeated.

83

"Oh, hello!" She suddenly seemed to notice Riley standing in the living room.

"Hey." Riley gave a little wave.

"Riley, this is my sister, Tess. Tess, this is Riley," Charlie said.

"Oh, the secret girlfriend!" Tess said with a knowing smile. "Charlie talks about you *all* the time. Mom and I love to tease him about you. Don't we, Charlie? Except this is the first time he's allowed us to meet you."

"Tess doesn't know when to shut up," Charlie explained to Riley, blushing.

"Well, I'm really glad to meet you and your mother, finally," Riley said, smiling at Tess. "I think it's really cool that you're into rescuing cats. Maybe I can help. I have some friends who might be interested in adopting. As soon as I get home, I'll start e-mailing everyone I know."

"Really?" Charlie's mother said, clasping her hands together. "That would be wonderful, Riley. Wouldn't it be wonderful, Tess?"

Tess was scribbling something down on her clipboard. "Definitely. I'm making a note to myself to follow up with you on this, Riley."

"You can call me or e-mail me anytime, Tess," Riley said. "Charlie has all my contact info."

"Fab," Tess said, continuing to scribble.

"Excuse us a moment," Charlie said to his mother and sister. He grabbed Riley's arm and steered her into a small TV room. Several cats were lying on the couch, preening their whiskers.

"Listen," Charlie whispered to Riley when they were alone. "Now do you understand why I wasn't exactly dying to have you over here?"

"You should have just been straight with me," Riley whispered back. "Your mom and sister are rescuing homeless cats! So what? That's way more important than having a picture-perfect house."

"Yeah, I guess you're right," Charlie said. "I never thought of it that way." He put his hands on Riley's shoulders and gazed into her eyes. "I'm sorry, Riley. I should have told you the truth from the beginning. Can you ever forgive me?"

Riley smiled. Then she stood on tiptoe and kissed him lightly on the lips.

"That means yes," she said softly.

Charlie smiled. He wrapped his arms around her, and they hugged for a long time.

chapter
eleven

"Close your eyes and bring your focus to your breathing. In . . . two . . . three . . . four. Hold, count to four. Out . . . two . . . three . . . four."

Chloe closed her eyes and followed the instructions of the yoga teacher, Star. Next to her Chloe could hear her father breathing to the count. He was an old pro at this.

On her other side, however, she could hear her mother shifting impatiently on her yoga mat. Her bracelets jangled every time she moved.

Chloe had decided to make a few more attempts to get her parents to appreciate each other's world before tonight's big romantic New Year's Eve. This morning she had convinced her mom to join her dad and her at the Kinetic Karma Yoga Center.

This was Chloe's first time at Kinetic Karma, too. It was a large, sunny studio filled with dozens of earnest-looking yoga students. Incense smoke wafted through the air. A portable CD player emitted what sounded like the low, repetitive drone of chanting monks.

"Make your breath gurgle slightly in the back of your throat," Star called out. "Imagine that you are breathing in the ocean with each breath.

"What is she *talking* about?" Macy asked Chloe. "Breathing in the ocean? How can that be possible? We'd drown, wouldn't we?"

"Remember, it's important to be very quiet and focus inward on our breathing while we're in class," Star said.

Chloe winced, knowing that the instructor was directing her comment at Macy.

Chloe heard her mother grumbling under her breath. Then she fell silent. Chloe continued her breathing exercise, relieved. Maybe her mother would behave and get into the spirit of this class after all.

"Let's all meditate for the next few minutes," Star suggested. "Continue with your breathing, and clear your mind of all thoughts, all clutter, all mental and emotional debris."

Chloe breathed. She tried to clear her mind. But she kept thinking about tonight. The champagne was chilling in the veggie bin. The menu was all set. Riley was picking up flowers, candles, and romantic CDs at the mall.

Now all Chloe had to do was get her parents to enjoy it. She had told them that she and Riley wanted to prepare a New Year's Eve dinner for the four of them, to make up for Christmas. Their parents had agreed. Little did they know that an intimate dinner was planned for two, not four!

Still, her parents' relationship had not exactly been heating up on schedule. The blackout, the Surf Expo, nothing was going as planned. Chloe hoped that this yoga class this morning would help her mom appreciate her dad's laid-back world and personality a little more. And this afternoon Chloe had a plan to do the same for her father.

Star clicked off the CD player. The room was completely silent as the students fell into their meditation.

Clear your mind, Chloe told herself, breathing slowly and deeply.

She heard a jangling sound to her left. Chloe opened her eyes slightly. Her mother was punching buttons on her cell phone, checking for missed calls and messages.

"Mom!" Chloe hissed.

But it was too late. The instructor walked over to Macy's mat.

"I'm afraid you're going to have to leave," Star whispered to Macy. "We have a strict rule against cell-phone use during classes."

Macy smiled apologetically. "Oh, I'm so sorry. No problem! Thank you for the lesson."

Macy leaned over to Chloe and Jake. "Bye, guys.

Thanks so much for bringing me here. I haven't felt this relaxed in months!" she whispered.

Then she gathered her things and walked out of the class, her cell phone glued to her ear.

Chloe turned to look at her father. He was breathing deeply and shaking his head, as if to say, *Same old Macy!*

Chloe sighed. How was she going to get her parents to see eye-to-eye before tonight?

"And now I'd like to introduce to you one of the business leaders of our community, Macy Carlson!"

Mr. Lopez, the president of the Chamber of Commerce, shook Macy's hand as she walked up to the podium. Chloe beamed proudly. Her mother looked so beautiful, so professional. The room broke into loud applause.

"So this is what your mother does in her spare time," her father whispered to Chloe.

Chloe had dragged her father to the annual Chamber of Commerce holiday luncheon. Her mother was the keynote speaker. Chloe hoped that by seeing her mother shine in her role as a leading local business person, Dad would be able to better appreciate her goal-oriented, ambitious personality.

"Thank you all for being here," Macy began. "Today I'd like to address a subject that is near and dear to all our hearts: How we can expand our town's business base in an economy that does not encourage business expansion."

Chloe glanced at her father. He looked totally confused. He also looked a little lost in the sea of business suits and two-hundred-dollar haircuts. As usual he was dressed in casual mode: faded jeans, leather sandals, and a T-shirt that said *Love Animals— Go Vegetarian*.

Macy went on talking about tax breaks and joint advertising campaigns. Chloe picked at her prime rib. Jake nibbled on a roll, looking bored.

"It's not even whole-grain bread," he whispered to Chloe. "And this so-called butter is full of preservatives and chemicals."

"Did you try the mashed potatoes? They're pretty good," Chloe whispered back.

"They make that stuff out of industrially processed dried potato powder. They're not even real potatoes," her father complained.

"Oh." Chloe grimaced.

When Macy's speech was over, the crowd broke into another round of applause. "Are you a new Chamber member?" a woman at their table asked Jake.

Jake shook his head. "No, I'm here with Macy Carlson. This is our daughter, Chloe."

"How fabulous!" the woman said. "And what do you do . . . Jake?" she asked, peering at his name tag.

"Macy and I used to be partners in our own fashion design firm," Jake replied. "But I got out of the business.

90

I'm trying to get back to living simply, without all the craziness and conspicious consumption that goes with the territory. Mostly I read and meditate and try to figure out my place in the universe."

"How fabulous!" the woman exclaimed. "Have you ever considered writing a book about your experience? Maybe doing an infomercial? There must be some way we can bottle your lifestyle choice and make it available to all these harried, unhappy people out there!" She pressed a business card into his hand. "I'm an entertainment agent. Call me! We'll do lunch!"

"Okay, I'm out of here," her father whispered to Chloe as soon as the entertainment agent struck up a conversation with someone else. "This place is giving me a massive headache. I need to go home and meditate for a while."

"But what about Mom?" Chloe asked him, feeling a wave of panic come over her.

"What about her? She looks plenty busy." Jake nodded at Macy, who was exchanging business cards with a group of people at the coffee and dessert station. "I don't understand how she can do this day after day after day. Constant networking with no meaningful solitude is the most impossible existence I could ever imagine!"

Chloe frowned unhappily. That was *not* what she had wanted to hear out of her father's mouth.

Now everything depended on tonight. Otherwise Project Mom and Dad would be history!

chapter
twelve

Champagne on ice. Check. Roses. Check. Oysters on the half shell. Check. Candles. Check.

Chloe glanced at the table one last time. Everything looked perfect.

"Cole Porter or Billie Holiday?" Riley called out, punching buttons on the CD player.

"Cole Porter. Mom loves Cole Porter. Rile, where are the champagne flutes?" Chloe asked her.

"Don't panic. I'll get them."

Chloe took a deep breath. Relax, clear your mind, she told herself. Mom was upstairs getting dressed. Dad was on his way over. Everything was ready.

But would everything go as planned?

Chloe and Riley intended to get their parents all set up for their romantic reunion. Then the girls were going to go to a New Year's Eve party with Lennon and Charlie at their friend and next-door neighbor Larry's house.

The doorbell rang. "It's Dad!" Riley cried out.

"I'll get it!" Chloe said.

Chloe rushed to the door and opened it. Her father was standing there, holding a paper bag. He was wearing the same jeans and T-shirt he'd had on earlier.

"Happy New Year's, girls!" he said cheerfully. "I brought some wheat-free oatmeal cookies I thought we could have for dessert," he added, holding up the bag.

"Thanks, Dad!" Chloe said, taking the bag from him.

"Mom! Dad's here!" Riley called upstairs.

A few minutes later Macy came down the stairs. She was dressed in a floor-length black gown and matching black sandals with rhinestones on them.

"Whoa, Mom!" Riley said. "You look amazing!"

"Doesn't she look amazing, Dad?" Chloe said, smiling hopefully at her father.

"Of course she does. You should be careful in those heels, though, Macy. They're no good for ankle support," he pointed out.

Macy glanced at Jake's old, beaten-up leather sandals. "Since when did you become an expert on footwear?" she asked with a laugh.

Jake held up his hands. "Just trying to help. Anyway, great dress! Happy New Year's!"

"Same to you," Macy said. She pecked him on the cheek, and he pecked hers.

That didn't look like a very romantic kiss, Chloe thought worriedly.

"Quick, play the Cole Porter CD," Chloe whispered to Riley. Riley nodded.

"What's this?" Macy asked, glancing at the table set for two. "We're short two place settings. And where did you get the champagne?"

"Manuelo," Chloe explained quickly. "Riley and I thought that, uh, maybe the two of you could sit and enjoy a glass of champagne while we cook."

That is, maybe you could sit and enjoy a glass of champagne while we slip out the back door and leave you two lovebirds alone, she said to herself.

"Champagne doesn't really agree with me," Jake said. "Unless it's organic. They're making organic wines these days, you know."

"Oh, Jake, give it up." Macy sighed. "This is New Year's Eve! Can't you loosen up just once?"

"Loosen up? Look who's talking about loosening up! I bet you can't make it through dinner without taking at least three overseas business calls," Jake shot back.

Chloe and Riley exchanged a panicked glance. This was *not* working out.

"I happen to run a business with very important international clients," Macy said, putting her hands on her hips. "That's something you never appreciated. Well, welcome to the real world, Jake Carlson!"

"If that's the real world, I'm not interested in it!" Jake said.

Chloe held up her hands. "Okay, stop! I give up! I don't know how you two ever made it through a romantic dinner at Chez Sophie!" she exclaimed.

"What?" her parents asked in unison.

Riley frowned. "You know. Your big romantic date at Chez Sophie. On December seventeenth," she reminded them.

Jake and Macy stared at each other. Then they burst out laughing. "You thought we were . . . Oh, no," Jake said after a moment.

"We took our friends Seth and Mimi Maxwell out to celebrate their twentieth anniversary," Macy explained.

"What?" Chloe said incredulously. "What about the flowers from the Black Iris?"

"How did you know about those?" her dad asked her. "I got them for the Maxwells. Your mother thought it would be a nice idea. Which it was," he added.

"Why, thank you, Jake," Macy said with a smile.

"What's all this about, anyway?" Jake asked Chloe and Riley.

Chloe glanced at Riley. Riley shrugged, as if to say, *The gig's up.* It was obviously confession time.

"You guys better sit down for this," Chloe said to her parents.

She told them the entire story from the beginning: how she'd found the piece of paper with the address of Chez Sophie on it, the Black Iris receipt, the "blackout," the family outings, the vibe she was picking up from Dad that he missed Mom and their life together.

"I made up those e-mails from Jake246, Mom," Chloe admitted. "I know it was an awful thing to do. I'm sorry. It's just that I really wanted to help you guys get back together. I thought that's what you wanted!"

"Oh, Chloe," her mom said. She reached over and gave Chloe a big hug. "We really appreciate what you tried to do, honey. But your dad and I are—"

"—happy doing our own thing," Jake finished.

Macy nodded. "We're friends, which is exactly what we want to be right now."

"And who knows about the future?" Jake added, smiling at Macy.

Macy smiled back at him. "Who knows? But for now we like our lives—apart."

Chloe hugged her mother, too. And then she hugged her father. "So everything's cool?"

"Everything's cool," Jake told her. "Now let's open that bottle of champagne—organic or not!"

Chloe watched as her father lifted the champagne bottle out of the ice bucket and tried to pop the cork without success.

"Oh, Jake, give me that," Macy said. "You never did know how to open them. . . ."

Everything was back to normal. Which was how it was meant to be.

"Happy New Year," Charlie whispered to Riley.

Riley smiled at him and kissed him on the cheek. "I'm so glad you're here," she whispered back.

Riley glanced over at her parents, who were sitting on the couch and laughing. They were watching a New Year's Eve special on TV. In the kitchen Lennon and Chloe were microwaving some popcorn.

Lennon and Charlie had come over to take Chloe and Riley to Larry's party. Soon it would be midnight—time to go next door and leave the parents to toast the New Year together, as friends. But everyone was having such a good time at the Carlsons', Riley wasn't sure they'd make it to Larry's.

Charlie glanced up at the ceiling. Riley glanced up, too. She suddenly realized that they were standing under a sprig of mistletoe.

"I think that means I get to kiss you," Charlie said softly.

"I think you're right," Riley replied, blushing. She glanced over at her parents. Their eyes were glued to the TV set.

Charlie leaned over and kissed her on the lips. Just then Riley felt something hit her head. "What was that?" she exclaimed, backing out of Charlie's arms.

"The mistletoe," Charlie said, leaning down to pick it up. "Someone didn't tape it up too well."

"Blame it on Manuelo," Riley said, giggling.

Lennon and Chloe came out of the kitchen, bearing a bowl of popcorn. "Who's hungry?" Lennon called out.

"Bring that over here," Macy said.

"Is it organic?" Jake asked.

Macy threw a pillow at him, which Jake ducked, laughing.

"Rile, help me bring out glasses for the sparkling grape juice," Chloe called out to her.

"No problem."

Riley joined Chloe in the kitchen. Chloe handed her a few pretty crystal glasses.

"So this night wasn't a total disaster after all," Chloe said, grinning at Riley.

Riley giggled. "No. Actually, it's the opposite of a total disaster."

The two of them stood in the kitchen doorway, taking in the scene. Lennon and Charlie were chowing down on the popcorn and talking about their favorite bands. Dad was telling Mom a joke, and the two of them were cracking up.

Everything was good, Riley thought. The Vail trip had been cancelled, but she and Chloe ended up having a great Christmas at home. Riley and Charlie had almost broken up, but they were back together again, and their relationship was stronger than ever. And Lennon and Chloe were supertight, as always.

And even though Project Mom and Dad didn't work out, their parents seemed happy.

"Ten-nine-eight-seven-six . . . " a voice rang out from the TV.

"Five-four-three-two-one . . . Happy New Year!" Riley, Charlie, Lennon, Chloe, Jake, and Macy cried out in unison.

Loud whistles and cheering came from the TV audience. Then Riley saw something amazing. Her parents exchanged a kiss. A major kiss.

Wow, Riley thought. That's a pretty romantic kiss for "just friends."

She and Chloe stared at each other with knowing smiles.

"Is this the best New Year's ever or what?" Chloe whispered to Riley.

"Definitely the best," Riley agreed.

so little time

Check out book 17!

the makeover experiment

"**R**iley Carlson and Charlie Slater—" said Dash Gilford, flashing a television host's megawatt smile, "you've been selected to appear on *Total Teen Makeover!*"

"Oh, wow!" Riley gasped as the other couples in the room applauded. "Really?"

"Absolutely!" Dash grinned.

Riley couldn't believe it! She and Charlie were going to be one of four couples featured on a special teen episode of her favorite television makeover show. Television cameras would follow each couple around for a week. First the guys would be made over according to their girlfriends' directions—clothes, hair, the works. Then the couple would be filmed going on dates and hanging out with friends. At the end of the week, the television audience would pick the couple they liked best.

[Riley: Not that I want to change Charlie for good. After all, Charlie likes himself the way he is, which is punk—music, clothes, attitude, everything! But it would be a kick to see him dressed in something besides grunge for a change!]

Riley gave Charlie a hug. "Isn't this cool? I can't believe it!"

"Me neither," Charlie said. He was smiling, but Riley could tell he was less than thrilled. "Seriously, I *can't* believe I'm going to do this."

"Believe it, Charlie." Dash laughed. "Starting tomorrow at the mall, you'll begin your transformation from punk to California Cool."

Charlie rolled his eyes.

"Oh, man, *Pacific Male*?" Charlie exclaimed the next day at the mall. As usual, he was wearing black jeans, black combat boots, and a black T-shirt with the logo of a band Riley had never heard of. Charlie stared at the trendy men's clothing store as if it were a monster about to devour him. "Please tell me we're not going here!"

Riley nudged him in the arm and smiled brightly. "Remember, we're being filmed," she murmured, nodding her head toward the TV camera in front of them.

"But *Pacific Male*?" Charlie almost whimpered. "Like, could it be any more *mainstream*?"

"That's what we like about you, Charlie," Dash Gilford laughed. "You say what's on your mind!"

Dash and his assistant Miri stood on either side of Dave the cameraman, a young, bald guy with a thick red beard. With them were two more members of the crew, in charge of sound and lighting. All of them wore *Total Makeover* T-shirts.

They'd drawn a crowd the minute they arrived at the mall and it kept getting bigger.

"Come on, this place is great!" Riley insisted. "It has all kinds of cool stuff."

"She's right, Charlie," Dash assured him. "And don't worry—we won't ask you to try on any three-piece suits."

"Is that a promise?" Charlie asked, smiling half-heartedly.

"Ha!" Dash laughed. "Is that a promise, Riley?"

Riley nodded eagerly. "Definitely!"

"You heard her, Charlie," Dash declared. "Come on, let's go shopping!"

Riley took Charlie's hand and walked with him past the camera into the store. Trailed by the crew, the two of them began checking out the clothes.

[Riley: Actually I checked out the clothes. Charlie just made a beeline for anything black.]

"Okay, I'm coming out," Charlie called from the dressing room forty minutes later. "I don't suppose you can turn the camera off."

"Ha!" Dash chortled again.

"I didn't think so," Charlie muttered. "Okay, here goes."

Wearing dark tan khakis and a soft, dark red shirt, Charlie stepped out of the dressing room.

[Riley: Wow!]

"Wow!" Miri echoed Riley's thought. "You clean up nice, Charlie!"

"Great choices, Riley!" Dash exclaimed. "Charlie, what do you think?"

Before Charlie could answer, the salesman poked his head into camera range. "Very nice," he commented. He glanced at Charlie's black combat-style boots. "But the shoes absolutely have to go."

Riley nodded. The boots did *not* fit with Charlie's new look. "Right. Let's see some topsiders and tennis shoes."

Half an hour, three pairs of shoes, and six full shopping bags later, the entourage swept into *Hair by Max*, a trendy hair salon. Max himself, a handsome man with flashing white teeth, gazed critically at Charlie's long, unruly brown hair.

"I'm thinking longer in front than in back, and we'll let it fall naturally onto your forehead," Max said.

"No way, no cutting!" Charlie said, starting to stand.

Dash laughed. "He's right, Max. Just style it."

Max looked disappointed. But then he brightened. "Some gel here, and I'll push this part back over your ears, and soften it with the blow-dryer. And as a final touch, some temporary highlights."

"You mean like, purple or something?" Charlie asked hopefully.

"What about it, Riley?" Dash asked. "It's your call, remember!"

Riley shook her head. "Purple's too punk for your new look," she told Charlie. "It'll just be lighter brown in places. It'll look great, you'll see!"

Max's assistant whisked Charlie away for a shampoo and, five minutes later, whisked him back to the chair. With Dave filming, Max went to work painting the highlights onto Charlie's hair. Then, after a session with the blow-dryer, Max spun the chair around so Riley and the crew could get the full effect.

[Riley: Double-wow!]

"Lookin' good, Charlie!" Dash declared. "Definitely California Cool!"

"Oooh, yeah!" a voice called out sarcastically. "Want us to start calling you *Charles*?"